HITLER

THE TERMINAL BIOGRAPHY D. HARLAN WILSON

RAW DOG
SCREAMING
PRESS

Hitler: The Terminal Biography © 2014 by D. Harlan Wilson
ISBN: 978-1-935738-58-9
Library of Congress Control Number: 2013920629

First Paperback Edition, February 2014

Cover Design by Matthew Revert
www.MatthewRevert.com

Headliner No. 45 Font by Kevin Christopher
www.KCFonts.com

Raw Dog Screaming Press
Bowie, MD

www.RawDogScreaming.com

PRAISE FOR THE WORK OF D. HARLAN WILSON

"Provocative entertainment."
—*Booklist*

"A bludgeoning celluloid rush of language and ideas served from an action-painter's bucket of fluorescent spatter."
—Alan Moore

"New bursts of stream-of-cyberconsciousness prose."
—*Library Journal*

"Wilson writes with the crazed precision of a futuristic war machine gone rogue."
—Lavie Tidhar

"Wacky experimental fiction."
—*Publishers Weekly*

"Fast, smart, funny."
—Kim Stanley Robinson

"Pomo cybertheory never tasted so good!"
—*American Book Review*

"Utterly original."
—Barry N. Malzberg

"If reality is a crutch, Wilson has thrown it away."
—*Rain Taxi*

ALSO BY D. HARLAN WILSON

For Alois Villafuerte.

"Since, however, his whole being still has too strong a smell of the foreign for the broad masses of the people in particular to fall readily into his nets, he has his press give a picture of him which is as little in keeping with reality as conversely it serves his desired purpose. His comic papers especially strive to represent the Jews as a harmless little people, with their own peculiarities, of course—like other peoples as well—but even in their gestures, which seem a little strange, perhaps, giving signs of a possibly ludicrous, but always thoroughly honest and benevolent, soul. And the constant effort is to make him seem almost more 'insignificant' than *dangerous*."

—Adolf Hitler, *Mein Kampf*

CHAPTER 1

This book is not about Adolf Hitler, the German dictator, mass murderer, art school reject, cocaine and methamphetamine addict, and so forth. I called it *Hitler: The Terminal Biography* so you would buy it. Everybody likes to read about Hitler. I won't mention him again. Go to the next page please.

CHAPTER 2

I don't know what this book is going to be about yet.
Next page.

CHAPTER 3

I thought of something.

A girl in a plaid dress cries about the loss of a doll. She approaches me for help and I realize that she is a doll. Dolls need dolls too. And desire is the desire for desire. The object-cause of desire can never be obtained. If it is, you are DEAD.

I should mention that need and desire, while interconnected and to some degree co-dependent, are altogether different experiences and require different modes of negotiation and parallax. But I'm unhappy with the direction of this story. Specifically, I don't like the girl-as-doll artifice. I don't know why. It belongs to juvenilia, or trivia, or manga. I don't care for the present tense either. Furthermore, I deploy the keynote term *desire* (trans. *Wunsch)* five times in four lines. This is preceded by a usage of the less encumbered term *doll* four times in three lines.

There is a question of effort. Of labor. Of aberrant and subjective industry.

And spontaneous overflows of emotion.

It is good to be clever but cleverness should be muted and buried in the sand. Nobody should be able to detect it but me.

CHAPTER 4

Lacanian psychoanalysis is a nice way to enter into a discussion of identity and the politics of subjectivity but perhaps not the best vehicle to jumpstart a biography, or a novel, or any "entertaining" book-length project. Nonetheless we will employ Lacan for this very enterprise. One always writes what one knows.

Apparently the French psychoanalyst and theoretical rockstar didn't like to stop at red lights. He sequestered graduate students and minor lecturers to chauffeur him around Paris in a refurbished Lincoln Town Car, but always-already on a trial basis, because they only lasted as long as they could avoid encountering and obeying red lights, nightmarish articles of signification.

I remember the day after such an incident. By "remember," I refer to the acquisition of mnemonic runoff collected in this case by Jacques-Alain Miller, Lacan's protégé and longest-running chauffeur.

Distressed, Lacan regarded Miller in the rearview mirror with a glare that seemed to suggest: "Of course you are not the ego-ideal onto which I project the primordial sap of my otherness." Then he got out of the car and walked into oncoming traffic, storming across the street like a man on a mission of vengeance.

There were collisions and a pileup, but Lacan made it to the other side of the street unscathed and kept marching forward towards the university. Miller pulled up and tried to coax him back into the Town Car. Lacan ignored him and marched the rest of the way to the Faculté de Droit at the Panthéon.

Later that afternoon, he somberly paced to the lectern. He shuffled through his notes and played with his knuckles for awhile. Finally he said: "We need to kill the gangster. The gangster of language. A multitude of depictions, of rivalries, of suspicions and affective games lurches across the periphery. The alchemical properties of syntax render us the enemies of wine and cheese. And alchemy is tantamount to conspiracy."

This seminar has yet to be translated into English.

CHAPTER 5

"I'm on the ledge! I'm going to kill myself!"

I was in fact on a ledge and I had a knife. But I had no intention of committing suicide. She broke up with me and I felt bad, though. I cried out as if stabbing myself.

"I'm stabbing myself! There, and there! G'bye."

I called her back five minutes later. "I'm sorry. I shouldn't have done that. I didn't stab myself. I don't plan to. Can we just talk? Let me tell you my side of the story."

She didn't want to hear it. Her decision was final. I had been a rebound. She didn't even like me and she wasn't really attracted to me. She hadn't intended to be so candid but I forced her tongue. She wanted me to leave her alone. She wanted me never to call her again.

"I'm stabbing myself!"

I hung up and called back.

"Please stop calling me."

"Why do you keep picking up the phone? You pick up the phone, like, every time."

She hung up. I called back and she answered the phone again.

"I'll be over in a few minutes. We need to talk about this. Seriously. I think we can work it all out."

She said she'd call the police if I came over. I made a compelling objection and she agreed not to call the police. I submitted a riveting appeal and she agreed that she might actually like me. "I might even love you," she added. By the end of the conversation she insisted that we move in together. At the very least, I needed to come over and see her, but I decided to stay home. Better off without her.

CHAPTER 6

All right I know what I'm doing now. Apologies for the false starts.

I can promise you transparent prose and the meaningful rhetorical device of anaphora—a speedy reading experience, if nothing else. And no Hitler.

I can't promise you anything else.

CHAPTER 7

Adolf Hitler was like any other boy. Full of energy and imagination. A categorical awkwardness rendered him the target of ample bullying, and he endured systematic beatings, some of which put him in the hospital for weeks at a time. His mother was his greatest comfort. For years, critics debated whether he got the idea for the goose-step (trans. *Stechschritt*) in the wake of a beating as a way to demonstrate power in the face of his oppressors, throwing his legs into the sky with egregious finesse, or whether his mother somehow planted the idea in his head as a way of loosening the joints and strengthening the calves and thighs in order to, one day, demonstrate a kind of corporeal prowess, even in a static, standing position; regardless of context, nobody would be able to disrepute the primacy of his legs. Both are credible accounts of origin, but no records, letters, diaries, etc. exist to confirm the matter one way or the other.

CHAPTER 8

When I get on a plane, I assume that nobody wants to die. Especially the pilot. I recognize the prospect of terrorists and hijackers but generally they don't concern me; the chances of being terrorized or hijacked on a plane are slimmer than winning the lottery. Statistically you're safer in a plane than you are in your bedroom. What concerns me is the pilot. Does he care about me or not?

As I stepped on board, the pilot shook my hand and said, "I'm not like the others."

Like airplanes, like life.

CHAPTER 9

"Hey, wait up there! You! Stop right there!"

The man was, like, way down at the bottom of the hill. It looked like a quarter mile or so but it couldn't have been that far.

I said, "It's raining, asshole! I'm not waiting for you! I don't even know you, you dumb motherfucker!"

It was true. It was raining and I didn't know him, although I remembered passing him in the street. He had a dog on a retractable leash.

He yelled at me again. I decided to wait for him.

He might have been fifty or so. I don't know; I can't tell how old people are. He had a cane and some wrinkles, but not too many wrinkles, and the cane may or may not have been a fashion accessory. He looked kind of weak, though, so I assumed he was older, and that means he was probably pissed off about something: the closer we get to death, the angrier we get about dying. Still, I didn't do anything to him.

"What's your problem, redneck?"

Gripping a tattered umbrella that looked like it had exploded out of his fist, he accused me of nearly running him and his dog over when I passed them in my Mini Cooper a few minutes ago. I told him I didn't come anywhere close to hitting them. Also, since they wouldn't move out of the middle of the road, I had to drive across somebody's front yard to get around them. There must have been more than ten feet between us.

"That's just what I'm talking about!" he shouted, waving the cane in a preemptive circle with one hand as he pumped the umbrella up and down with the other. The dog growled and barked and bristled its wet fur. I remained silent, stoic. The man reprimanded me, gesticulating at the Mini Cooper on the top of the hill. I tried to be mindful of the raindrops falling onto my face and skull. After awhile the man admitted that I had done nothing wrong and he was just jealous of the Mini Cooper, a top-of-the-line Super Model Convertible Roadster. But I had already forgotten about him.

CHAPTER 10

Two hours later I arrived at the charity auction in Dublin, Ohio, a quaint town with crenellated brick buildings just north of Columbus, the capital city and by far the best thing the state has to offer in terms of culture and bourgeois amenities, which isn't saying much. The weather had cleared up in tandem with my mood. The weather always follows my mood.

Before the proceedings, I bussed about fifty homeless people to an IHOP for brunch. They sort of trashed the restaurant but everybody got enough to eat and I tipped the waitresses heavily to make up for all of the Badness. Back at the auction, I donated an undisclosed six-figure sum to further research into the genetic catalysts of narcolepsy (currently unknown) as well as more mainstream donations like to Planned Parenthood and the NRA, organizations that I have strong feelings for in their own rights despite their polarized political affiliations. Then the auction began.

I purchased an intricate ivory sculpture for $19,950 after a bidding war with a man who looked like a bassoon. I don't condone elephant murder and mutilation but I didn't like my opponent's wan, knobbed face. My only option was to win. It was the largest purchase of the evening and afterwards the chamberlain invited me onstage to address the attendees.

As a former debate team coach and all-purpose crowdpleaser, I am a proficient speechmaker. I imparted the following words:

"Sometimes everything reveals itself as a victim of clarity. This can be good and this can be not so good. It's good to be able to make meaning. But meaning can hurt. Mostly it hurts. We might say the same thing about truth. We might say the same thing about idiocy. But if you're an idiot you probably stopped reading *Hitler: The Terminal Biography* after the first chapter, so you're in the clear. Remember: *you are the author of your own victimization*. You may apply this apothegm to any aspect of your demolition."

I exited in a whorl of indecision.

CHAPTER 11

An airplane takes off and explodes. Another airplane takes off and explodes. They consider shutting the airport down. Another airplane takes off and explodes. One of the planes explodes at the gate. Now they're starting to get worried; the airport should probably be shut down at this point. A plane explodes as if to confirm their canny hermeneutic. Better call the Boss, they say.

They call the Boss.

He answers the phone and he can't hear anything but explosions and static and some screaming and choking. Crank call.

He hangs up the phone and calls the airport and the airport explodes.

"Did you just call this number?" he asks.

The airport explodes again, plane parts and fireballs arcing into the sky. "Jesus Christ what's going on over there?"

He hangs up and goes to work. The airport is in ruins. There are no planes left and the terminal tower flails in the wind like a car dealership balloon-man. Everybody's stuck on the top floor. The Boss tries to save them with various ropes and ladders and makeshift dumbwaiters but nothing works. In the end, everybody spontaneously combusts. It's only the Boss now. Him alone. Him and nobody else. He drives around the tower for awhile and then the car runs out of gas and comes to a slow, quiet stop.

CHAPTER 12

Until this morning, I have never had to use my seat as a flotation device.

The plane crashed into the Potomac.

It actually wasn't that bad, although the Potomac is filthy, and people were burning and drowning and so forth, but I swam ashore, paddling my legs and hugging the seat to my chest, and I crawled onto the Parkway without a scratch.

The crowd at the Lincoln Memorial looked at me like I were a fallen god. Even the statue of Lincoln seemed to regard me with a certain deference.

Drunk on power and adrenaline, I hailed a cab and went to Bowie to see my publisher.

"I crashed," I told the editor-in-chief, "and I survived. See? I might have been the only one who lived. It'll make a great book. I'm alive."

The editor-in-chief motioned for me to be quiet. She was reading the manuscript I brought her. I had zipped it into my seat cushion when the plane was going down and saved it.

She finished reading and made a face. "Could you go out and weed the back patio? There's, like, a lot of weeds growing in between the cobblestones. I'll be out in a minute to help and we can talk."

I drank a screwdriver to calm my nerves. Then I went out back.

She came to check on me about a half hour later. "Geez," she said. "There's weeds all over the place. What've you been doing out here?"

I apologized. I'm a good weeder but I got distracted by a grapevine near the toolshed.

I sat on a tree stump and finished my cigarette. "I got tired. Gimme a break. I just got in a plane crash. I'm afraid to fly for Chrissakes. You know what that means? I'll never fly again unless I get back up in the air immediately." I gave her a once over. "Listen, I need you to throw me up in the air. Don't look at me like that. Just put your hands together and bend your legs a little and I'll do the rest."

She tried her best and I sort of got some air and I did half a backflip and landed on my rhomboids. I groaned for awhile. Then I got up and said, "That feels better. That's all I needed. Can you book me a flight to Australia for my first reading? They like me over there. This is assuming the book's ok. I'm sure it's fine. It's not my best work but that's the point. I'm confident readers will disregard, if not appreciate, my total lack of effort."

She had severe reservations about the book, namely the title. There was some back-and-forth and I had another screwdriver and a few more cigarettes. I decided to quit smoking on the spot. I do this from time to time. I didn't so much as think about cigarettes for nine months.

The editor-in-chief complained some more about the weeds and told me I couldn't go to Australia. I asked if Ohio would be better; they didn't like me as much there but they knew who I was and that's enough. She thought about it for awhile and eventually agreed on the condition that I cleaned the bathrooms inside and folded the laundry. Then we went to a Mongolian Barbecue with her husband and son.

CHAPTER 13

This evening I am as brazenly self-less as I want to be at any given moment.

There's one more thing.

I am as white as they come. And as black as they get.

CHAPTER 14

On my way to Ohio, the captain's voice passed through the intercom like a noxious barcode. "If you turn off the radar and fly around long enough," said the voice, "you're bound to hit something."

CHAPTER 15

Pregame strategy: To not try.

Endgame: To win. And to be as honest about myself as Dire Straights in their song "Money for Nothing" and William Wordsworth in his epic poem *The Prelude* despite obvious ideological incongruities between the band, the poet, and I.

Premonition: The eighth type of ambiguity . . .

CHAPTER 16

Maybe we could continue to explore the vicissitudes of air travel, bad writing, Lacanian antics, etc.

This is probably good enough.

I'll keep going for awhile.

I promise not to end on a clever note or by way of some clever artifice. You know I mean what I say even as I use the term *clever* twice (three times now, once in italics to underscore its role as a signifier) and make no effort whatsoever to vary and dynamize my language. Here are your shriveled desires on a dinnerplate. I have put the least amount of effort into this book as possible. As evidenced so far, my publisher has employed a big font as well as wide margins to fill out more space. This will emerge as a book yet. And I will slip into past and present tense without the slightest regard for form, caché and fluidity. I regret some things (e.g., the use of highfalutin words like *parallax*, *hermeneutic*, *cach*é, *highfalutin*, etc). You have thanked me by reading this far. You can thank me again by moving along to greener pastures.

CHAPTER 17

Welcome to a greener pasture. Congratulations. Cheers. Thank you.

Keep going please.

CHAPTER 18

There's a common misperception among the general public that writers make a good living. This isn't true. It's in fact morbidly untrue.

The average annual income for a "professional writer," whatever that means, is $5,000.

Nearly all of the writers I know have fulltime jobs they hate. They keep the jobs to make ends meet. In their spare time they do their writing and hope to land The Deal That Will Set Them Free, i.e., to sign a contract with a Big Publisher for a Big Book Deal that will allow them to quit the jobs they hate and do their writing for a living. This happens about .01% of the time. Maybe less.

The stench of desperation is a default aroma.

Another common misperception is that writers are good storytellers. This isn't necessarily true. It's in fact unnecessarily untrue.

Then again, what constitutes a "good story" can be a highly subjective affair. And sometimes nobody can say if a story is "good" or "bad." A story is a story is a story. Like this one, which I extricated from the vehicle of somebody else's "real life experience."

My coworker suspected I wasn't doing my work. We had adjacent cubicles with crevices in the divider panels through which we could see one another using, in his case, a mirror, and in my case, a snake-cam. Lo-tech all the way, he didn't know what he was up against, and I recorded him spying on me for three weeks, then turned the footage in to my supervisor. My supervisor confronted my coworker and he denied everything. Technically there was no proof: the mirror had been destroyed. Yes, I had shot footage of him destroying the mirror, breaking it into pieces and disposing of it in a trashcan, but it takes about a year to fire somebody from a government job with all of the paperwork that needs to be done. So my supervisor moved my coworker into a separate room all by himself. The room is big and has several conveniences, including a window and a private bathroom. But I haven't seen him in almost a year.

Obviously this account is just a template. The story as it would appear in, say, a magazine or journal of science fiction would look rather different. There would have to be a palpable element of cognitive estrangement galvanized by an intrusive and operable novum (e.g., AI, the Singularity, an alien invasion, psionics, linguistic devolution, etc.). Even in non-SF diegeses, characters would have to be developed with backstories and dialogue. More context is needed. (Where do they work? How did the characters end up working there? What's the weather like outside? Do people take walks at lunch? If so, when do they have time to eat?) More people of color need to be involved too and possibly a sexual deviant and a murderer or a drug addict. Maybe the coworker could spontaneously combust into a Burning Man at some point, feeling the pain of burning to death, but never burning to death; he would simply keep burning, awake and alive and agonized, and everything he touched would go up in flames. But does it really matter? Again, a story is a story is a story. Some people will like it no matter what form it takes. It is only an issue of *mots disposés à la page.*

CHAPTER 19

I recall Don DeLillo's *White Noise* in which Professor Jack Gladney emerges as a scholarly Führer by way of presiding over a cutting edge Hitler Studies program at a fictional Midwestern university known as The-College-on-the-Hill.

White Noise is the only other book about Hitler that will be invoked in *Hitler: The Terminal Biography*. No need to actively bind and gag my own thunder.

CHAPTER 20

It doesn't matter what I write from now on. You know I've tricked you and you're still reading *Hitler: The Terminal Biography*. Whatever I write, and however I write it, you're probably going to think it's pretty good.

I'll try to stick with the themes I've introduced (e.g., aerial trauma, civil rights, the rise and fall of the Third Reich, doll culture, weed control, the insolvency of writers, the Burning Man, etc.) and develop them in compelling ways. This is what a lot of authors do. Despite certain Machiavellian impulses, I want to be like everybody else. Homogeny exacerbates my raw pandemonium but anything is possible in the realm of biography.

I'm running out of ideas.

CHAPTER 21

So maybe, like, a sex scene here. Hetero—to maximize the collective *jouissance* of my readership, most of which isn't gay, since most human beings aren't gay, and generally I don't write for a gay readership. It doesn't matter how the scene's written. Somebody will get aroused. I learned this at a science fiction convention. I was on a panel with a tall muscular black man who had really black skin that frightened me it was so black. His teeth weren't as white as you'd expect. The whites of his eyes were jaundiced but not quite yellow or even ocher.

"That's shitty writing," he told the audience in reference to a pornographic, heterosexual-friendly passage from a novel written by Virtually Every Writer.

"Yes," I agreed, "but who the hell cares? Half of America will make a mad dash to the toilet for a jerkoff when they read that. Most of America. Everybody in the universe. I mean, if I say, like, I don't know . . . TWO PEOPLE ARE FUCKING ON THE COUCH!!!" I screamed it as loud as I could a few times. I strained the cords of my neck and it felt like my larynx ruptured but I could still talk. "If I say that . . . [cough] . . . excuse me . . . if I say that, I'd clear this room out, assuming we weren't discussing the potency of fuckwords, any fuckword, genital-oriented or otherwise, in which case anybody who gets up and leaves looks like a weirdo." A few people got up and left. I sneezed. "Well. You know what I mean. I think it's a pretty clear point. Totally indisputable too. It's kind of stupid that you mention the writing's bad. Of course it's bad. It's a book. Books are fuckin' crap. All of them. Isn't this common knowledge? Have you ever read a good goddamn book? Seriously. Writers are total fuckin' dummies. So are publishers and editors. Obviously. Right? I don't know. I just think your comment was . . . reckless? Well, really very dumb anyway. You should think a little before you undo the latch on your maw." I had been drinking scotch since 9 a.m. and was more or less sober.

"That's shitty writing," reiterated the black man.

CHAPTER 22

Here's a passage from a story I wrote called "Abattoir." The ellipsis does not symbolize the omission of any content.

Courtesy reminder: . . . handle the inscribed *esprit de finesse* with extreme care. Failure to pollute the waters of Irk with your corporeal referendum may incite mortal, oozing sex wounds. This is not a test. The university reputation survey applies to everyone that falls into the aforementioned demographic and must be processed and completed in a timely fashion. Mind the office partitions on your way to the gas chamber. Inhale the content. Die.

"Abattoir" appeared in *WTF?!*, an anthology published by Pink Narcissus Press. Great name for a press. There is nothing fictional about the story. Nor does subjectivity enter the equation. Per usual, the absence of outspoken bias reigns supreme.

CHAPTER 23

Storytime! Title: "Six Word Sci-Fi."

"Mechanical flâneurs goose-step across the prairie."

This is the first story in my book *They Had Goat Heads*, the best collection of my short fiction in print to date. It was inspired by an issue of *Wired* that featured six-word science fiction stories by prominent science fiction authors.

This is a tragedy.

I swore I would never write a book about writing and being a writer, and I'm even breaking the rules of formal composition and using the second person, a no-no according to the constraints of my identity-rubric and, for that matter, MLA style and the world according to Strunk

& White. I've always hated it when writers write about writing and especially themselves. Writers aren't interesting. At best, writers are straw dogs.

There is a difference between being a writer and being an author (see chapter 10 of *Freud: The Penultimate Biography* for an explanation). Likewise are there good *artistes* and bad *artistes*. More on this later.

I have decided that *Hitler: The Terminal Biography* will be a textbook for writing. And, *ipso facto*, bodybuilding.

Tragedy averted.

Nothing can be done about the mind. The body is another matter.

This textbook may be full of insipid, throwaway minutia but it'll all come together in the end and *Hitler: The Terminal Biography* will definitely teach you a good deal about bodybuilding. I am a bodybuilder.

All attempts to define my physique fall short of the actual physique. My physique preempts descriptive and figurative language with the towering phantasmagoria of its gaze. Let us simply agree that my physique is "shredded" (an industry-standard term for otherworldly muscular definition) from neck to ankles.

The first, most important rule of bodybuilding is: DON'T BE OBESE!!! You don't have to be. Stop eating so much food. In subsequent chapters, I will tell you how to eat right. Remember: 90% of revising your physique is contingent upon good nutrition whereas only 10% depends on physical exertion even if the latter is an essential component of the revision process.

I want to bridge the realms of bodybuilding and literature. The practitioners of both realms don't have a brain in their heads, but there must be some technique of mediation. I intend to find it. In this capacity, I will approach and embody the übermensch. I mean Nietzsche's übermensch, not Hitler's post-Nietzschean perversion, which he extrapolated for Nazi empowerment. Bear in mind, Nietzsche didn't lift weights. I don't think he even went on walks. He certainly didn't practice good nutrition. Hence I must somehow out-Nietzsche Nietzsche.

Next chapter.

CHAPTER 24

The problem with writing conventions is I always get too drunk too soon and stumble around the hotel with my social filter switched off. In other words, I tell the truth. Worse, I focus on everybody's shortcomings, pointing them out and parodying them for effect. Mine above all. Then I pass out in the hallway or the party maven's couch or somebody's bed and do it again the next day, although, barring incapacitating hangovers, I typically work out in the morning in the hotel gym before I dive into the old Punch Bowl.

This is a workout I did one morning at the last con I attended. Chest and legs are the focus and I do supersets for nearly everything. Ideally the first, primary exercise is done so that I fail or come close to failure on the final rep; the second, supersetted exercise, on the other hand, is always done to failure. (DB = Dumbbell. SM = Smith Machine. BB = Barbell. MC = Machine. DS = Drop Sets.)

DB Bench Press superset w/DB Flye
1x12 1x10 1x8 1x6 1x12
SM Incline Press superset w/Pushup
1x12 1x10 1x8 1x6 1x12
BB Decline Press superset w/Cable Cross
1x12 1x10 2x6-8
Weighted Dip superset w/Pec Deck
1x12 1x10 2x6-8
Hack Squat superset w/MC Leg Extension
1x12 1x10 1x8 1x6 1x12
MC Leg Curl
4xDS
Sitting Calf Raise superset w/DB Calf Walk
4x10-15
Ab Circuit
10-15 min.

I do the ab circuit at the end of every workout, every day, performing whatever exercises come to mind, and only resting as I move from one exercise to the next. These generally include various permutations of plank poses and crunches and leglifts with the assistance of kettlebells.

Each superset is preceded by one or two high-rep warm-up sets. I also do five minutes of moderate cardio on the stationary bike, elliptical or treadmill to get loose before each workout, and afterwards I do anywhere from 10-45 minutes of intense cardio, depending on the length of my workout, which in its entirety ranges from 45-120 minutes. As for pre- and post-workout nutrition, beforehand I eat one medium-sized banana, one tablespoon of honey, and 2.8 oz. of solid white albacore tuna. Afterwards I drink a protein shake containing no less that 40 grams of whey or casein protein and some kind of fast-burning carb, typically a starch like white bread or jasmine rice, but foods with dextrose in them (e.g., Haribo gummy bears) work too. I won't explain why this formula works since it's common sense to any reasonably informed bodybuilder and you can always figure it out by picking up a fitness magazine (e.g., *Muscle & Fitness*, *Iron* Man, *Flex*, etc.) and reading it for a few minutes since all fitness magazines regurgitate the same information and what you need to know is right there in every issue.

The rest of the day I eat lean beef, chicken, fish, eggs, vegetables, fruits (mainly berries), nuts, small portions of natural oils, brown rice and sweet potatoes—whole foods only. My macronutritional consumption of these foods is about 300-150-50, i.e., 300 grams of protein, 150 grams of carbs, and 50 grams of fat. While monstrously ripped and encrusted in veins, I'm too skinny and need to increase both my fat and carb intake. It's difficult to eat enough, though, if whole foods are your only source, even when you consume 6-8 meals a day.

On nights that I drink I don't eat anything. I count calories, of course, and I know that 5 oz. of red wine and its counterpart in vodka or scotch (1 oz., a modest shot) amounts to about 120 calories. Curiously, there are no carbs in alcohol and, in spite of the health benefits of red wine (no more than 5-10 oz. per night), alcohol contains nothing but empty calories. To manifest and maintain a cut-up physique, you should only drink alcohol on Friday and Saturday nights. Get plowed if you want. Five days and nights out of the week, you should remain completely sober and drink about a gallon of water per day. Smoke weed or take Xanax or Ativan if you need a fix. There are no calories in marijuana and benzos.

Stay away from "100% fruit juices." They contain too many calories and aren't as "healthy" as the companies that make and sell them would have you believe. Drink water and eat real fruit instead. Don't eat too much real fruit, though, because most non-berry fruit contains too many calories and should be reserved for breakfast and pre-workout consumption only.

No carbs at all after 6 p.m. Preferably 4 p.m.

Finally, supplements. I don't really believe in them but I take a few anyway. Pre-workout: 8 capsules of BCAAs (GNC Amino Complex 4400). Post-workout: 2 tablets of creatine (GNC Amplified Creative 180) and 2 capsules of L-Glutamine (any brand as long as you're getting 1500 mg per serving). The L-Glutamine actually works wonders; basically I don't get sore the next day because of it. I also take 3-6 mg of melatonin before bed to help me sleep on nights that I don't get drunk. More than 3 mg tends to give me a headache in the mornings, and I've read that taking more than 3 mg doesn't really help, i.e., 3 mg does the same work as 6 mg or even 9 mg. But there's always placebo to consider.

Incidentally, I advise against buying supplements at actual GNC stores. With hardly any exceptions, the people that work there are aggressive idiots who presumably live on commissions and they hound you throughout your entire shopping experience. Their sales pitch: "Do you want something cheap or do you want something that works?" My consumer retort: "So you sell things that don't work here?" Etc. In any case, if you must shop at GNC, I recommend knowing exactly what you want when you go in there and talking on your iPhone, loudly, the entire time, to a real or a fake person. But you're better off getting your supplements online at somewhere like Bodybuilding.com or even Amazon.com. That way, you abjure the middleman, a fabricator of pain and suffering and, at the very least, annoyance.

CHAPTER 25

Somebody sent me a picture of their kid. "This guy just melts my heart," said the caption.

"He looks like a fuckin' homunculus!" I observed.

It was true—dented head, amphibious eyes, broken-in-half grin. Somebody had to say something.

CHAPTER 26

This chapter should foreground the plight of German citizens and conflate it with the cultural exploits of African Americans in order to reflect the title of the book and my angle of incidence. But I worry at this point about my dune-filled facial expression, about the phenomenology of my nose and the sloping recalcitrance of my eyes.

Speech. Speech.

I had forgotten where I was and who the audience was and I wasn't altogether sure who I was but I remembered myself quickly and in any case my auto-pilot takes care of everything. I said, "The topic this evening is a curious one and I must admit that I enjoy curious topics. Where am I? Well let me just say that it feels good to be somewhere.

But you've all paid the price of admission and so you're entitled to some form of knowledge and entertainment. That's my thing, per se—the purveyance of knowledge and entertainment. Well so I should get started." I cleared my throat for awhile. The microphone shrieked like an electric wraith. "Well so there I was strangling a Mormon. Make no mistake: Mormonism is a bona fide cult but I don't have anything against Mormons or cults unless they kill people or infect people or get in my way. Anyway I didn't know he was a Mormon until later but he said something to me about coffee that I didn't like and I just kind of reacted and so forth. Everybody got worried and there was a big to-do but in the end it all worked out and nobody died and I didn't go to jail. I rarely go to jail. Moral: Don't strangle Mormons. Or do. It all depends on where you do it and who's watching, you know? Well that's more or less what happened and I'm a better person for it." I think that's what my auto-pilot said, and meant to say. It made sense to me and the audience seemed to enjoy it. There was more to the speech but I recall getting bored and when I get bored I shut down. A period of awkwardness preceded a greater period of awkwardness. I could tell that the audience was rooting for me to go on. But that was it and I thanked everybody and left with an enthusiastic plug for *Hitler: The Terminal Biography.*

CHAPTER 27

My publisher decided to send me into the future, or into the past, or just on a long space trip, but like I said, I'm a drinker, and while I don't drink as much as some other authors and celebrities, I drink enough to cultivate a need on a weekly basis, so they had to fill me with alcohol every few days to keep me asleep. Here is the science fictional element of the narrative. But everything is science fictional. Consider any of Sandra Bullock's movies. They rotoscope her voice onto her mouth and so forth.

(Further references to, disquisitions on, and/or explications of Hollywood iconography, blip culture, futureshock, terminal identity, cybernetic meat puppetry, etc. will be subverted to the best of my abilities. We may assume that Hollywood, blip culture, futureshock, terminal identity, cybernetic meat puppetry, etc. are normative conditions.)

I should probably return to Lacan—he returned to Freud, after all—who I invoked in the fourth chapter, or thereabouts, but I was still figuring things out back then, and Lacanian psychoanalysis and linguistic certitude, for me, is the altar on which everything is erected. It's sufficient to mention him in the beginning of *Hitler: The Terminal Biography* and move on from there, allowing the epiphanic formulae, the coded withdrawals to lock into position.

CHAPTER 28

To Berlin, then.

I booked a flight with AirFreud. Business class.

I drank four screwdrivers and ate a bag of almonds. The flight attendant was loud and kind of rowdy and violent, but in a nice way. We talked about the good gay bars in Baltimore and Zurich and I told him how Gertrude Stein was a racist. He said black people were overrated and I said, "I love white people." The remark created a sort of toxic impasse. We tried to overcome it, but the dye had been cast, the cat drowned in a trough.

I met the Boss at the gate.

In the interest of character development, he told me his name was Alois Villafuerte.

"Somebody's got to make the hard decisions," Alois Villafuerte reminded me, shaking my hand. "Not everybody can bear the burden of leadership."

I told him that was a good point and we spoke for awhile in German about schedules, tour dates, meet-and-greets, and other procedures. I didn't understand any of it. I don't speak German. But you only need to latch onto a few German words and shout most of them out, like you're upset, or passionate, or deranged, and people will think you're as German as anybody. Even Germans.

We took a stretch Volkswagon to the first bookstore, Schropp Land & Karte, which wasn't so much a bookstore as a beer hall.

I ordered a plate of mussels and a pint of Hefeweizen. People were waiting for me, but I hadn't eaten in awhile and needed to get something in my stomach.

Alois Villafuerte sat next to me and watched the food come off of my plate, the beer come out of my glass.

An hour or so later I prefaced my first reading with the following disclaimer: "Hello. Thank you for having me. I am very happy to be here. Let me begin by saying that if you take a picture of yourself with your pet cat or your pet dog—like, if you have a picture in your wallet or your purse with your pet, right now—I'm just not going to like you. I apologize in advance, but I'm serious and correct when I say that people and their pets are for the birds. They're animals, mind you. I understand that you fail vis-à-vis human contact and socialization, but sublimation of your insecurities onto domesticated vermin is as deplorable as it is absurd and ridiculous. Is that clear? I don't know if I can make it clearer. But I can try."

That didn't go over well and a lot of people left. Then I gave a speech about beer, foregrounding German dominance, and I filled the empty seats and generated a kind of lazy mosh pit in the front. Nobody understood my reading because I did it in English, but I gesticulated and inflected my voice in such a way that everybody loved it.

CHAPTER 29

A Famous Author was on his deathbed. He had drank, smoked, and eaten too much throughout most of his adult life and fifty-year writing career, and he perceived physical fitness as a ludicrous enterprise the very mention of which undermined his intellect. Why should he focus on his body when his mind could tapdance across the hardwood of genius?

"You focus on the betterment of your mind," I once told a neophyte writer who offered me the same line of horseshit. "Why is it that you don't focus on the betterment of your body as well? The mind is the prison of the body and the body is the prison of the mind. I don't write and pump iron for kicks. My objective is to beam Divine Rays into the Ass of Eternity."

The Famous Author looked like a scorched, deflated cow poured onto a slab.

Diverting the attention of a nurse, I slipped into the hospital room and knelt at the author's side. I had on a tight Spandex outfit that accentuated my musculature in all of the right places and produced a formidable vascularity on my arms and neck.

"Please," I begged. "I need a blurb before you die. Look at my cephalic vein. The name of my book is *Hitler: The Terminal Biography*. You don't even have to read it. Just say something nice about it. Please. I love your writing. It has been so inspirational to me over the years."

I had never read anything by the Famous Author. I don't read fiction.

The Famous Author replied, "Thank you, my son. I wish . . . I . . ."

He choked and died.

I hurried downstairs and left the hospital and got in my Mini Cooper and drove to Bowie, Maryland, spur-of-the-moment. I delivered the blurb to my publisher in person and this time we all went to a sushi place I liked. I ordered a dish called "miriami": squares of sashimi tuna and salmon draped over small balls of sticky brown rice. Almost the perfect bodybuilding food. The protein content was a bit low, though, so I added three Protein Freeze margaritas.

The blurb worked.

Hitler: The Terminal Biography became a bestseller and I talked endlessly about my relationship with the

Famous Author at signings and readings during the interstices of speeches. I often quoted the blurb as I stood on the hood of my Mini Cooper, which was small enough for me to drive into most major bookstores and park behind the table they had set up for me.

"I wish . . . I . . . ," I often said.

CHAPTER 30

What I've written so far has been accomplished in one sitting at my home theater while watching the first season of the original animated version of *He-Man & the Masters of the Universe* on Netflix. I'm not going to revise what I've written and I'm never going to read it again.

Momentum will not be siphoned in any way from the Jewish experience.

I am certainly siphoning momentum from Hitler's reputation as one of recent history's most imposing villains.

To reiterate: the title of this book is a marketing strategy. Some of my books have become bestsellers and I don't need to worry about money, but I'm addicted to the Game.

Point of order: my bloodline is not without its Jewish phenotypes let alone its African phenotypes. In accordance with the laws of western cultural etiquette, I can essentially do what I want vis-à-vis WWII and so forth.

The scope of Hitler's evil is by no means unparalleled, but it is by all means remarkable.

You will not leave this narrative diegesis without taking away information that you have never received before in any other book on Hitler—and not on Hitler. *Hitler: The Terminal Biography* comprises an utterly unique assemblage of word hordes. You will only experience the likes of these word hordes here.

My objective is precisely the same as any diligent and earnest rapper's: to talk about myself, to assert my "I," to give voice to my real and fictional desires, and to sculpt and carve an identity out of the shimmering mire of my wonderful life. This is an exercise in dignity. And if you have ever listened to, say, gangsta rap, you can't deny that what I'm doing is much nicer, friendlier, cleaner, holier, and gentler.

CHAPTER 31

The leaves fall from the tree. More leaves fall from the tree. It's nice out. One likes to watch the leaves falling. They're falling everywhere. One imagines the leaves kissing the grass, leaf after leaf, and forming into a great pile, and then one lights the pile on fire and rolls through it in an effort to avoid the flames. One succeeds. On the other side of the pile, things looks pretty good. That's a good burnt-up pile, one tells oneself, and those are good burnt-up leaves. One especially likes the way in which the leaves have burnt, ashes mounting into a fallen vector. A baby is born. It's me. I've looked better but I don't look bad. The mother lies on the hotplate, evicted. I grow up. The mother remains on the hotplate. I try to help her off. She likes the hotplate. So does the father. I get older and hit somebody with a car. One wonders who it is. One buries the body in the woods. Years later they find the body. The father is elderly now. Clutching his back, he helps me prepare a formal statement. The glands hang from the ceiling of the courtroom on thick arterial tubes. They are enormous and grotesque glands and even the judge can't take his eyes off of them. The glands fall from the ceiling. Only the father disregards them, gripping his knees and whispering to himself, "Little people, little problems. Big people, big problems." The glands fall from the ceiling. More glands fall from the ceiling. It's humid in here. One wishes the glands wouldn't do that. They're falling everywhere. They're exploding against the floor of the courtroom. Surges of tissue and mucous antagonize the jury. One forgets about the body. Constellations evolve into unfamiliar patterns. I am elderly now. In the future there is no Law and no Nature. In the future the act of scratching is devoid of sound. A fallen vector rises out of the afterbirth. One attempts to climb atop the vector and stand there like a pariah. One succeeds.

CHAPTER 32

Name of a character, possibly an alternate protagonist:
Bartholomew Scratch.

CHAPTER 33

Bartholomew Scratch waits in the waiting room and gets bored after awhile. He gets up and goes to the magazine rack and thumbs through it for what seems like forever. Eventually he finds a swimsuit issue in which the women aren't wearing swimsuits and in fact are being penetrated by hairy goliaths. What the heck kinda swimsuit issue is this? Scratch wonders as he turns and turns the pages.

He had to hand it to the women: they were very toned and kind of muscular, but not anabolically enhanced, and obviously they did lots of cardio. He didn't notice the men's bodies so much other than the hair and certain peculiarities of stance and physiognomy. He wished they would go away and sort of leave the women alone.

"Bartholomew Scratch?"

By the time they call his name, he has experienced certain mindwaves and left the waiting room.

He goes to a studio to find the women in the magazine. They're in the powder room. He waits around all afternoon for them to come out, but they leave through another door, a back door, and nobody tells him about it.

He returns to the waiting room. The door is locked and there's a note on it that says he's not allowed to come back in because he left without fulfilling his obligation as an occupant of the waiting room.

The note explodes. The door explodes.

Scratch walks inside and the waiting room explodes. The explosion infects his legs. The legs don't explode, but now they definitely contain the kinetic potential for an explosion; he can feel the chemical reactions and the origins of supersonic shockwaves in his calves and knees and thighs; any moment may be the moment of an extinction event, of total fragmentation, if not vaporization.

He walks away very carefully and doesn't look back, worried that his vigilance will set eternity in motion.

CHAPTER 34

Bartholomew Scratch isn't working out. I am going to kill him now.

There will be a long description of the death scene including outtakes and alternate endings as well as prefaces and forewords and introductions and codas and afterwords written by informed and prestigious intellectuals. You will judge the gory passing of Scratch based more upon his supplements than on his selfhood and my construction thereof.

CHAPTER 34: REDUX

I'm going to do chapter 34 again. I have no modus ope-
randi other than my piddling malaise.

Weary of coming up with ideas and frankly of writing
altogether—this might have been, like, two or three years
ago—I cut-and-pasted a few randomly selected Wikipedia
articles (e.g., "African American Vernacular English,"
"Boeing 777," "Weimar Republic," "*It's A Wonderful Life*,"
"Cloaca," etc.) onto the same document, sent it to my
publisher, and told them to call it *The Doves of Greed*.
It's ok. There are publishers now who compile various
theme-related Wiki entries into book-length form. People
love it. Here's an excerpt from the sixth chapter of my
effort, "Surgeon General of the United States":

Responsibilities

The Surgeon General reports to the Assistant Secretary for Health (ASH), who may be a four-star admiral in the United States Public Health Service Commissioned Corps (PHSCC), and who serves as the principal advisor to the Secretary of Health and Human Services on public health and scientific issues. The Surgeon General is the overall head of the Public Health Service Commissioned Corps, a 6,000-member Commissioned Corps of the USPHS, a cadre of health professionals who are on call 24 hours a day, and can be dispatched by the Secretary of HHS or the Assistant Secretary for Health in the event of a public health emergency.

The Surgeon General is also the ultimate award authority for several public health awards and decorations, the highest of which is the Surgeon General's Medallion . . . The Surgeon General also has many informal duties, such as educating the American public about health issues and advocating healthy lifestyle choices.

The office periodically issues health warnings. Perhaps the best-known example is the Surgeon General's Warning labels that can be found on all packages of American cigarettes. A similar health warning appears on alcoholic beverages.

Originally *The Doves of Greed* was only supposed to be published as an ebook, but it sold so well the publisher put out paperback and hardcover editions. It continued to sell despite readers getting wise to my bullshit. Market research showed that my name was enough to instigate the flows of consumer desire. This prompted me to call my next book my name. Another hit. I pursued this authorial line of flight to its natural end, i.e., to the point where ennui sunk in its proverbial fangs. It was at this juncture that I began research on *Hitler: The Terminal Biography*.

CHAPTER 35

When I am dead and idle I am confident that I will be remembered precisely for the reasons I want to be: my talents as a biographer and the vascularity of my physique. As you stand over my grave, the words SCHOLAR and BLOOD VESSEL will flash onto your mindscreen, signifying my identity, my grief, my elliptical supremacy.

CHAPTER 36

This is going to be a long chapter. I will start with my first kiss and proceed with meticulous care through the ascension and evolution of my sex life up to the present moment.

CHAPTER 37

Once I sue the police, I can get a nose job and become a professional rapper.

Losing steam now. And interest. Give the next chapter a try.

CHAPTER 38

Still not much happening. Do you feel cheated?
Remember: Godzilla's roar is copyrighted.

CHAPTER 39

But every chapter in which nothing happens is another chapter I don't have to write. And yet it fills space and functions as a chapter. This is good for my project. In my own private utopia—the only viable utopia, of course, being subjective—I will stand on the Precipice and do nothing, not even stand there, and everything will fall into the Golden Bowl of my Lap.

CHAPTER 40

An airplane takes off and explodes. Another airplane takes off and explodes. They consider shutting the airport down. Another airplane takes off and explodes. One of the planes explodes at the gate. The gate explodes. A few clouds explode and so does a tract of blue sky. Now they're starting to get worried; the earth should probably be shut down at this point. The earth explodes as if to confirm their canny hermeneutic. Better call Alois Villafuerte, they say.

They call Alois Villafuerte.

He answers the phone and it's his mother. She sounds like his father but it's definitely his mother. "Goodbye, son," she weeps. "God bless you."

There's a Big Crunch followed by a Big Bang that brings us back to the moment when the first airplane takes off and explodes.

Alois Villafuerte has a hunch that something's wrong. He calls his mother and she connects him with the airport.

"Did you just call this number?" he asks the switchboard operator. But it's not the switchboard operator. It's a representative for AirFreud.

He hangs up and goes to work. The airport seems fine. The planes are working and the terminal tower rises into the clouds like a self-possessed phallus. Everybody's eating lunch on the top floor and the air traffic controllers are having a cocktail party. Alois Villafuerte joins them and in the end everybody gets quite drunk. Alois Villafuerte likes the feeling. He's not an alcoholic, per se, but there's no denying how much he likes the feeling of drinking alcohol in excessive quantities. Inspired, he drives around the tower for awhile and then the car runs out of gas and comes to a slow, quiet stop.

CHAPTER 41

An airplane takes off and explodes. Another airplane takes off and explodes. It keeps happening.

"I'm going to put a stop to this," says Alois Villafuerte, an inconsequential player but a capable and somewhat gifted player.

He gets in an airplane and starts to fly around the sky. It explodes.

He parachutes to the ground and gets in another plane and it explodes during takeoff, just before leaving the ground. He rolls to a stop on the runway and gets really mad. He tries to fly two airplanes at once and they crash. He eyeballs an airplane and it explodes. People glance in his direction.

He attempts to fly the airport into space and the airport explodes. People are really looking at him now, expecting great things despite his well-known identity and existence as a Little Man.

Alois Villafuerte takes a handful of beta-blockers to cope with all of the attention and the ensuing stagefright. "Good lord that feels better." But he's out of drugs now and worried about the next time he might suddenly become the apple of an audience's eye. He calls the pharmacist and the pharmacist explodes. Better call a doctor, they say.

They call a doctor.

The doctor shows up at the AirFreud check-in booth in a doctor's uniform asking if anybody's seen Alois Villafuerte anywhere. An AirFreud attendant who only serves business class customers kindly asks him to step aside since he didn't book a business class seat. The doctor becomes enraged and demands to see the president of the airport.

"Is there a president of the airport?" asks the AirFreud attendant who only serves business class customers.

The doctor says whoever runs the airport will be fine.

"I don't know who runs the airport. I think airports just run themselves."

Alois Villafuerte hangs up and decides to go home. The airport has seen better days but he's done all one man can do. The planes and the doctor are on fire and the AirFreud attendant who only serves business class customers has retreated to baggage claim to talk to her friend at the Hertz car rental booth. Alois Villafuerte puts on aviator sunglasses and puts down the cartop and drives through the tall green hills with one hand on the wheel and one elbow resting on the carside. It's a beautiful day out and the sky looks beautiful and the wind blows through his hair and he feels the sun on his face and smells the transcendent freshness of the ocean surf far below.

CHAPTER 42

Alois Villafuerte's doppelgänger's face keeps turning to alabaster. He's driving down a busy highway and he can feel the transformation every time it happens. He looks in the rearview mirror and taps his cheek with a fingernail and the mask of alabaster cracks and falls to pieces in his lap. He continues to look in the mirror. Everything seems ok. The moment his eyes return to the road, though, he feels his face harden and turn to alabaster again. He looks in the mirror and taps his cheek and sheds the mask. Same thing happens again. It keeps happening for, like, hundreds of miles. He tries to focus on the radio but music doesn't offset reality. Finally he pulls into a rest area to clean all of the maskpieces out of his Mini Cooper.

"Where'd you get that Mini Cooper?" asks a tourist.

"The source," he says. "Great Britain. The British Motor Corporation. The shareholders of the corporation made it for me themselves. With their own hands. I insisted. This is the only one like it. There will never be another Mini Cooper like it."

The tourist starts to drop elbows on car, moving from the front to the back, from the hood to the roof to the trunk and back onto the hood and then he nails the driver's side mirror and takes it off. The driver's side airbag explodes and the reverberation from the blast sends the tourist backflipping across the parking lot into a granite trashcan, spraining his limbs. He lies on the sidewalk and moans. Alois Villafuerte's doppelgänger goes inside the rest area to use the toilet. He presses the button on his keychain to lock the doors of the car on his way in. He figures that everything will be all right if he lets a few minutes go by.

There are a lot of people in the bathroom and he gets stagefright. All of the stalls are occupied but there's an open urinal. He goes up to it and allows uncomfortable, ultraviolent episodes to run across his mindscreen and dissuade his attention from the act of urination. It works like a charm. He holds his hands under cold water and dries them beneath a turbopowered blowdryer and goes back out to the car.

It's gone.

The notched body of the tourist lies in the dispossessed parking space.

Alois Villafuerte's doppelgänger lies down next to the body and tries to start a conversation but the tourist doesn't say anything. He wonders who took his Mini

Cooper. He wonders whether or not he could live at the rest area for awhile. There are vending machines and they keep it pretty clean, although there's a lot of foot traffic and probably germs. Germs don't bother him that much but people do and he doesn't think living at the rest area for any reasonable length of time is a viable option. He wonders what to do next and suddenly the next chapter of his life yawns awake like a petulant leviathan.

CHAPTER 43

I write to support my teaching habit.

I am an Associate Professor of English at a satellite campus of the University of Fostoria. The Ludavico Campus, they call it.

Our faculty retention rate is unspeakable. It's a horrible place to work. There's only one African American, the gravedigger, and he grew up in Littleton, Colorado, one of the richest, whitest suburbs in America. He has the speaking voice of Charleton Heston.

Sometimes they ask me to sit on hiring committees. I usually ignore them, or I say that I'd be happy to sit on the hiring committees, then never show up to the meetings, embracing an aggressive modality of Total Absence.

My colleagues are primarily Amish. Many of them don't have beards, but I know they're having sex. Just last week I caught one of them in the computer lab railing a student on the CAD machine.

I like the Dean of the campus, though, and generally I do what she asks me to do.

"I need you to pick up this candidate at the airport and drive her back here so we can do the interview and all that," says the Dean.

"Ok."

I go to the airport.

The candidate is overweight and can't drive a car. I ask her why she can't drive a car and she says she's lived in the city all her life and there's no need to.

I say, "That's fuckin' bullshit," and I take her to the gym and scream at her through a blistering workout, then drive her back to the airport without bringing her to campus for the interview. I tell the Dean that she flaked out and wanted to go home.

The Dean reprimands me in soft tones.

I go back to my office, ease into my recliner, and fondly admire the gifted illustrations that my children have made for me. I've hung them on the wall between the plaques that boast my various degrees in higher education. I love my kids more than Ego itself. I would flush my truth-tellings down the toilet for their betterment. And I do. They know it. That's all that matters. Everything else is an out-of-the-corner-of-the-mouthism.

CHAPTER 44

Every book I have ever written begins with a passage arrogated from some other book or movie that contextualizes the work and serves as a beacon of inspiration. A lot of authors exhibit similar praxis and it's one way I can successfully contribute to the mission of sameness. We authors are all alike.

CHAPTER 45

The trainer broke out into song.

He wasn't a bad singer but he was definitely trying too hard and his face turned purple.

The bodybuilders didn't know what to do.

I took the trainer aside and told him about Lacan and the way in which his mind and by extension his body were interpellated by language. He understood perfectly and I became his mentor. I took advantage of his knowledge of nutrition and muscle development but I gave back everything he gave me in the form of hardboiled scholarship. We were inseparable for months. Soon I got him to drive me around in a limo and act as my chauffeur. We talked about the history of literary theory in the same breaths as we talked about the development of good pectoral and abdominal muscles.

One day we were out driving around and a light changed from green to yellow.

"Don't miss that light," I said, frantically pointing through the divider.

The trainer missed it. The light turned red. We stopped.

I got out of the limo and stormed into traffic.

Panicking, the trainer drove after me, but he lacked the expertise of a driver like, say, Jacques-Alain Miller. He squealed through the intersection and a truck smashed into the rear of the limo, exploding the gas tank.

CHAPTER 46

Artifacts delivered to your mailbox are by default meaningless, innocuous, and superfluous. If senders want to get you, they will get you electronically. This is common knowledge. *Communication for Dummies.*

Recently I hooked up a garbage chute to my mailbox and lent the same courtesy to my neighbors and now when the mail comes it goes straight where it belongs. The chute runs into the ground and empties into the bowels of the vulgaria at the summit of which resides my luxury *grand-bourgeois* home on a hill of thoroughly fertilized and finely trimmed grass and Feng Shui herbage. I mention this because printed mail had become a heavy psychological burden to me (tantamount to negotiating a GNC salesperson) and now that burden has been lifted even as my spirits more or less remain anodized among the same ghostly corrosions. I leave the rest in your capable hands.

CHAPTER 47

Something else worth mentioning: I know I've obtained prime condition when I'm comfortable scrutinizing my physique in ALL OF THE MIRRORS.

It helps that I have naturally dark skin and don't have to tan, but it's virtually impossible to maintain a full-blown rip without some fluctuation and softening. When it's time to get ripped (six or seven weeks out from a writing convention), I test my perception of myself in every mirror within a 20-mile radius (barring private residences). My wife tells me I have body dysmorphia. I think it's just a matter of being practical, self-aware, and truthful. Granted, nobody likes to hear or see the truth, which is why the purring specter of disavowal figures so prominently into the human condition. What I aspire to do is remove this specter, this optimum illusion that permits people to function and not feel terrible all the time. In my corporeal prime, they will see me, they will read me—and they will not be able to disavow me.

CHAPTER 48

"Hé, ta geule!"

There is no context for the exclamation.

"Will you do that for me?"

There is no context for the query. My eyes remain fixed on the dry ulcer as a vulture circles overhead.

It is an attempt to surmount the birth of stasis.

"Insert orifice here."

The context for the directive is palpable, winedark and obtrusive. Applying a Beowulfian death-grip to the webbed knuckles of the context will not memorialize the context or reify its misconstruction.

The colorless vegetable revises the junk. Go back and bare the hindquarters. Emaciated figures have collected the passengers and spread them onto a sloping basin. Decerebrate. Murmur something into the air vent and see where it goes.

A termination. A *Weltanschauung.*

Transept.

"I am not a man. I am dynamite."

The context begs for mercy, but the mercy-givers have punched out and gone to lunch. The truth is terrible. Flesh and genius is worse.

I can't speak for the rearrangement of ages.

CHAPTER 49

My wife claims that she caught the flu yesterday because a popcorn kernel got stuck in her throat and she couldn't get it out. Apparently this happens a lot to people, but I don't believe her. I hereby fossilize my disbelief for eternity via *Hitler: The Terminal Biography*.

CHAPTER 50

The Dean took offense to my forthrightness. Everybody does. But I was adamant. "I'm trying to do something else," I insisted.

The Dean looked at me. She liked me.

I said, "I mean, blackness isn't an affliction. Nor is semitism, another notable chain-link on the helix of my genetic code. I can write about the black experience. But really what matters is the human experience."

The Dean looked at me.

"All right. Well I got this great idea about Frederick Douglass. I want to write his biography. He wrote three autobiographies and a few other people wrote biographies on him, but I have a new angle that involves his sex life. I'm going to put him in outer space too. There'll be this floating slave plantation. Like Laputa or something. Only in space. My theory is that Douglass was a kind of sex pirate in his day and that a vast multiracial cult was erected on the platform of his guyparts, the prowess of which he developed in tandem with his intellect. Coupled with the element of science fiction, the biography is certain to become a *New York Times* bestseller. Written in my token Hörnblowér prose, it's bound to become a literary smash, uprooting academia, lifting its skirt and exposing a flavorsome achene, which is to say, the meaning of excellence. Everybody wins."

The Dean didn't like the science fiction angle, but I convinced her that it was the best angle to pursue, and she was happy to fulfill my request for a grant in the amount of $7,500 to perform research in Washington, DC, at the Library of Congress (home of the Frederick Douglass Papers), in England at the University of Liverpool library (home of the largest special collection of science fiction in the world), and finally in Talbot County, MD, where the infamous fistfight between Douglass and "slavebreaker" Edward Covey took place on a plantation that today exists as a spacious outdoor mall.

I took a university vehicle (free of charge including gas) to save on the cost of airfare and spent most of the grant on booze and spas. I didn't go to Liverpool. When I got back I made sure it was nighttime and I parked the university vehicle in the university lot and siphoned the gas that remained in the tank into my Mini Cooper.

CHAPTER 51

End of the semester. As always, students are mad.

One of them writes me an email and says, "I am disgusted that you did not get my final essay and that I received a D in your course. You—"

I delete it.

Another student writes me five 1,000 word manifestos explaining how the D I gave him was unfair and his grade worked out to a C despite the automated point system that calculates grades with absolute perfection. This is more than he's written all semester. I read the first sentence of each manifesto and delete them.

This incidentally is how I read novels and how everybody should read novels. The first sentence should be sufficient and contain the seeds, the sprouts, the trunk and the leaves and the distant stump of the entire narrative. If it doesn't, it's a bad novel.

CHAPTER 52

Have you returned to the first chapter yet to reread the first sentence of *Hitler: The Terminal Biography* and reassess *Hitler: They Terminal Biography*?

CHAPTER 53

An ideational mass preys upon my Ego.

Better do something about it: according to the AirFreud emergency pamphlet, the ego is the only viable medium, i.e., "We speak only to the ego, we are in communication with the ego alone, everything is channeled via the ego" (qtd. in Lacan, *Seminar I: Freud's Papers on Technique*).

For all of his ambiguous greatness, Lacan essentially reinvents Freud and by extension huffs on and polishes the coattails of the other big hermeneuticists of literary theory, namely Nietzsche and Marx. Freud apropos psychoanalysis. Nietzsche apropos philosophy. Marx apropos socioeconomics (i.e., class). These seminal figures are absolutely indispensable to a rudimentary understanding of structuralism and poststructuralism and ultimately to any intelligent comprehension of history as a symptom of any practical and/or pathological futurology. But Lacan's *desiratum* is Freud.

That information is indispensable to my project but really needs to be expanded and developed, unpacked and exegesized in another book. This is something I often tell my students, incidentally, when I make notes in the margins of their essays:

"Expand and develop. Unpack and exegesize."

I use bright red ink. My mentor in graduate school encouraged me to use green ink to mark up student papers because the color red possesses more negative than positive connotations whereas green fills students with a sense of freshness and hope and verve despite the content of the criticism.

CHAPTER 54

The only way to end this not-so-sleight-of-hand is with a speech. It's a short one.

I place my hands beneath the microphone and crack my knuckles. My knuckles don't run out of steam; I can crack them all and I don't have to wait for their cracking facilities to reboot. I build up to an aggressive crescendo of cracking that sounds like an apocalypse of popcorn, then decelerate and taper into silence.

Applause.

Deflation of my etched immediacy.

But maybe one or two more chapters to put some meat on the bones of *Hitler: The Terminal Biography*.

CHAPTER 55

Alois Villafuerte's doppelgänger doesn't like his name. He goes to the DMV to change it to Bartholomew Scratch. They won't let him. They don't say why. The doppelgänger becomes depressed. The depression intensifies when Alois Villafuerte ambles into the DMV in an attempt to get rid of his doppelgänger once and for all. They oblige him and after all of the paperwork is signed and processed the doppelgänger deliquesces and explodes into pulp confetti.

CHAPTER 56

Alois Villafuerte resides on the cusp of Futurity. Airplanes explode beside him and beneath him and above him as he strides down the Star-Spangled Corridor. He feels exceptionally powerful and loses himself in a tempest of solipsistic reveries that achieve a perfect storm. Then somebody calls him on the phone.

"Who is this?" Alois Villafuerte demands to know. "I can hear you breathing on the other end of the line and so forth." The *reductio ad absurdism* downgrades the register of his megalomania by at least five notches. Everything gets quiet and still and relatively peaceful.

Whoever is on the other end of the line remains on the other end of the line.

Alois Villafuerte doesn't hang up.

This goes on for awhile and Alois Villafuerte steps out of the Star-Spangled Corridor and looks for a café. Everything is closed, although he can smell fresh espresso. He follows the smell and it takes him to a reflecting pool that stretches out from the mouth of a great white church with a dome that looks more like an observatory than a church. But it's a church. He goes inside and asks the rectors and abbots and friars or whatever they are if there's espresso brewing and they explode, one by one, in slow motion, holy filaments expanding from a core of hard bone.

It is as if his voice incites the explosions, he realizes. He hangs up the phone and takes a vow of silence. But he knows his gaze is to blame too. So is his presence and even his absence. Alois Villafuerte can't save the world. Nor can he save himself. This epistemological certainty wounds him deeply. Grief-stricken, he worries that he won't be able to go on.

He feels better when he finds a café just west of the main cathedral.

It's empty except for an old man sitting near the window blowing on a small cup of soup. There are solid oak tables with cushioned seats. The baristas make good espresso and the café has a lot to offer in terms of scones and baguettes. Alois Villafuerte doesn't have much of a sweet tooth but he takes a chance on a lemon bar and he doesn't regret it.

CHAPTER 57

On behalf of myself, the Boss, Frederick Douglass, temporal rifts, the Surgeon General, vascularity, twenty or so screwdrivers, and hundreds upon thousands of aspiring malcontents, thank you for reading my book. Please be patient for the thrilling sequel, *Freud: The Penultimate Biography*, which should be available in a week or two.

CHAPTER 58

I sent the first 57 chapters (plus the chapter 34 redux) to my publisher and the editor-in-chief told me that there's no way they could publish the book at such a short length, even with the big font and the wide margins and all of the open space that precedes each new chapter title. I flew out to confront her at once.

"We have ethics, after all," said the editor-in-chief.

"There are rules and so forth," said the editor-in-chief.

"And truthfully it wouldn't be fair to readers," said the editor-in-chief.

I disagreed but there was no persuading her so I'm inclined to press on for awhile. For the record, it wasn't my idea, and I'm not responsible for anything that comes after the 57th chapter in terms of narrative cohesion and finesse. Subsequent chapters may or may not bear the likeness of feeble suckerpunches or, conversely, rictuses of belligerence. I'll begin with a slice of reality. Then I'll record a dream or something.

CHAPTER 59

I gave a free seminar for writers. I didn't want to but my publisher made me. Information was delivered on a point-by-point basis. Here's a synopsis:

1. Bleep.

2. Bleep.

3. Don't use writing as an excuse to embody a geometry of sloth.

4. Take a shower. Tuck in your shirt. Comb your hair. Brush your teeth. You there. Yes, you.

And you. You too. All of you. Good. Good. Good. Good.

5. Forget about the gym for now. Focus on diet. Eat one less meatball sandwich per day. We'll start hitting the gym when you lose some weight and your muscles can breath. The muscles need to remember that they exist, if only in an attenuated, wraithlike state.

6. Do not touch me. Ever. Assume my mind-body apparatus is off-limits. Pretend the apparatus is equipped with a default restraining order. I'm happy to sign books but keep your distance.

7. If you haven't already, check out my latest books, *The Kyoto Man*, a novel published by Raw Dog Screaming Press, and *Diegeses*, a collection of novelettes published by Anti-Oedipus Press. They're not my best work but they're all right.

8. Bleep!

9. Chloroplast.

10. Alois Villafuerte has eaten, like, eight lemon bars at this point. He can't stop. Also he drank too many espressos and he's having heart palpitations. He doesn't know what to do.

11. "Jouissance serves no purpose (*ne sert à rien*). Where there is being, infinity is required. There's no such thing as a sexual relationship. Stupidity nevertheless has to be nourished. Is everything we nourish thereby stupid? No. But it has been demonstrated that to nourish oneself is part and parcel of stupidity. What is at stake in analytic discourse is always the following—you give a different reading to the signifiers that are enunciated (*ce qui s'énonce de signifiant*) than what they signify. The cosmic theory of knowledge or world view has always made a big deal of the famous example of smoke that cannot exist without fire. Smoke can just as easily be the sign of a smoker. And, in essence, it always is. There is no smoke that is not a sign of a smoker. Everyone knows that, if you see smoke when you a approach a deserted island, you immediately say to yourself that there is a good chance there is someone there who knows how to make fire. Until things change considerably, it will be another man. Thus, a sign is not the sign of some thing, but of an effect that is what is presumed as such by a functioning of the signifier" (Lacan, *Seminar 20: On Feminine Sexuality*).

12. No Q & A.

CHAPTER 60

After all these years, my cousin comes out as a lesbian. She keeps saying the word "ejaculate" when she confesses to the family and even people on the street. The word has nothing to do with it. She isn't explaining how she ejaculates as a gay person or a formerly straight *poseur*. For her, the word functions as a discursive prop. Soon everybody in my family starts using "ejaculate" in casual conversation. It makes me uncomfortable, but I can't bring myself to ask them to temper their language for fear of exacerbating the already redolent air of discomfort.

We're sitting on the patio talking about the aphids that have died on the windowscreens. You wouldn't know they're dead unless you touch one of the corpses and it turns to dust in your fingers. Otherwise they remain attached to the windowscreens as if frozen in amber.

"There's no meat in the husks," I tell my sister. "There are only husks. Empty shells. Hollow membranes. Crusts without pieflesh. The molted snakeskins of the Void."

The doorbell rings like a pneumatic horn that somebody has stomped on.

It's my father and my best friend from high school, Scott Leete. Scott died years ago from choking on a virile marijuana roach.

They ask me to get my youngest daughter, Renee, and put her in the helicopter. She's two. Her eyes are so big and round they make surprised animé characters look like they're squinting.

It's not a helicopter. It's a cardboard shack onto which my father and Scott have strapped a propeller.

"Don't worry" says Dad. "We've done a lot of research and this is going to work."

We take off.

I strap Renee into a harness on the wall, but the floor comes loose and she's basically hanging in the sky by a string. She likes it. She talks babytalk. I take her off the harness and curl up with her on the floor, hoping the helicopter doesn't fall apart or explode. Dad and Scott sit in the cockpit and discuss viable modes of protraction and fiscal exhilaration. I focus on Renee and smell her aromatic babysoft skin and tell her how beautiful and smart and wonderful she is and how I'll always protect her no matter what.

CHAPTER 61

Here's how my wife interpreted the dream I wrote about in chapter 60. She's also an English professor at the Ludavico Campus of the University of Fostoria. We met in graduate school at a Halloween party. She wore a belly dancer costume and had gotten a spraytan. I dressed up like a lion tamer with a shiny red shirt, tight black pants, fake mustache and a whip. She had heard of me and my books and when she mentioned the name of one of my novels I fell in love with her immediately. We moved in together the next day and got married soon afterwards.

I have asked my wife to write her interpretation of the dream right here. I told her to write as much as she wants—the more the better. I even paused the movie I was watching in my home theater to go get her in lieu of sending a text message.

This is her interpretation:

(NOTE: I gave her five minutes to come up with something and she didn't do it. I told her that the longer she procrastinated the more I would cool off and lose steam in my quest to write like a derailed freight train. That's what she wanted, I guess. For me to fail at failing. So I . . . All right she's telling me to calm down and says she's got something now. I wouldn't get mad if she did what she said she was going to do.)

So this is my wife's interpretation (which I received via email weeks after I finished *Hitler: The Terminal Biography* and I'm going to cut and paste it here now):

First of all, your dream reveals your always too-enthusiastic investment in Freud. It's a classic castration complex dream—your female cousin taking on a male sexual role (something that obviously makes you feel displaced and insecure about your own masculinity), and then these purportedly alpha-male figures try to sell you a faux helicopter that, again, reveals your fear of the inadequacy of masculinity (yours, of course, but also the institution of masculinity altogether). The fact that it endangered Renee is less a sign of your fatherly affection and more a concern about your own ejaculation which produced her and the way that ejaculation and male potency is endangered by powerful women. That's my interpretation. But to be honest, it's not a very interesting dream, so

I'd like to tell you about a dream I had the other night. (And, yes, I understand that it's too heavily Jungian. I guess we all have our psychoanalytic affinities and trepidations.)

We had just bought our house, the one that we live in now, and we had moved all of our furniture in when I discovered an entirely new, unseen, unknown wing of the house. It was like a more contemporary version of Don Draper's apartment—it had all white furniture, though, and a full kitchen, with a spacious island in the center, terra cotta tiles, and a stainless steel double oven. A slightly grotesque mold ran down the walls, and I felt unsure about whether I could safely cook and prepare food with that mold right there on the walls. Nevertheless, I called your cellphone to tell you that we had a whole new kitchen, a huge one. I kept exclaiming: "We didn't even see this part of the house, but it's here!"

In the living room, a servant walked in. I'm a little unclear about this part. I'm not sure where he came from, but he was wearing a really tight black suit, like a wetsuit, kind of, but formal or something, and when I asked him about this part of the house, he said that the reason the real estate agent hadn't shown it to us is because this is where Mr. Grace, the former owner, murdered Mrs. Grace and that you could still see where their wine glasses had been. I looked. The wine glasses lay on the floor, rings of red wine still puddling in the bottoms. A plate of half eaten crackers remained on the coffee table between the white leather sofa and the white leather lounge chair.

I felt torn between excitement and disgust about this wing. I wanted to use the space because it fit so well with our aesthetic, but even in the dream, I knew that symbolically it was troubling. I don't care to analyze this dream further. I don't like what it seems to mean.

CHAPTER 62

My parents are obsessed with sunlight.

They bought a new condo recently, brand new, no updates or refurbishes needed, but one of the rooms didn't have any windows in it, so my father, an ex-globetrotter (from the 1960s crew), loaded the walls with dynamite and blew up the room.

"There's the sky!" he shouted from the rubble.

CHAPTER 63

I think this is good enough. If there are no more chapters after this one you'll know it's good enough. I invite you to return to chapter 57 now, where *Hitler: The Terminal Biography* was supposed to end, and then go back further to the first chapter and the first sentence and read it one more time to gauge the dynamism and acuity of the fully flexed physique of *Hitler: The Terminal Biography*.

CHAPTER 64

This is the publisher.

We felt that at least one more chapter was necessary.

We apologize for the methodology of the author and more or less everything about the author, but his books sell better than any of our other authors and he housecleans very well when he concentrates on the task at hand and isn't drinking and smoking or planning his next workout. "Every workout," he tells us, inhaling deeply, "must be carefully planned and documented."

We would like to take this opportunity to include the following stockroom disclaimer regarding the content of *Hitler: The Terminal Biography*. Imagine this disclaimer rolling down your mindscreen like the credits of a B-movie:

This has been a work of fiction. Names, characters, places and incidents are either products of the author's imagination or are used fictitiously. Any resemblance to actual events or locales or persons, living or dead, is entirely coincidental . . .

CHAPTER 65

This is the author. I'm sorry the publisher has ensured that *Hitler: The Terminal Biography* devolves into crass metafiction, something writers do as an excuse to circumvent the hard work of writing real narratives with round characters, intricate plots, seamless connectivities, upwellings of suspense, etc. As a matter of course, I want to mention that I am in opposition to the disclaimer remunerated in the previous chapter by the publisher if only for the fact that anybody who has read *Hitler: The Terminal Biography* this far (let alone reread the first sentence on multiple occasions) will feel the mortal impact of the disclaimer on their consciousness in the absence of its articulation.

CHAPTER 66

Alois Villafuerte dies. That's all anybody has ever wanted. Nobody knows how he dies but he's dead now. There are no explosions. There's no more dynamite. No more desire.

I had hoped to at least achieve 15,000 or maybe even 20,000 words, but it looks like this is the end. Perhaps widening the margins even more will satisfy and placate my readership. I leave you with the following adage that may or may not tie together the superfluities that punctuate this manuscript like the cross-bearing entreaties of a dogpoet . . .

CHAPTER 67

I think I can get 15,000 words. That's a good figure. I have a little over 14,000 now, maybe.

CHAPTER 68

I don't like what my wife wrote in chapter 61. Her interpretation of my dream is subjective and obviously plagued
by transference. It's possible that my interpretation of her
interpretation is just as subjective. Let's take a poll. Do you
like what she wrote? Please check the appropriate box:

☐ No
☐ No

(FYI I lifted this idea of speaking directly to readers and
asking them to check boxes from Donald Barthelme's
Snow White, a "novel" that also prefigures the "Exploding
Airplane Chapters," but only on the level of anaphora.

By no means does the present work constitute an act of plagiarism or, for that matter, postmodernism, the lowest form of Giving Up. I am more than willing to give up, and I have indeed given up, but only in a way that combines apathy with greatness.)

CHAPTER 69

This is your wife.

Indeed?

You can't combine apathy and greatness. It's physically impossible.

Also, there are two NO boxes. Ha ha.

I don't know why you want to write a book called *Hitler: The Terminal Biography*, no matter what it's about. That's distasteful and frankly mean. I won't even mention the quote at the beginning from *Mein Kampf*. Are you proud of yourself? It's not like we don't have enough money. There are your student loans, of course, and you spend way too much of our income on alcohol, cigarettes and weight equipment every month. I won't say how much because you get so mad about it. The point is we're doing very well. We have a big house in a nice neighborhood and you have a man-cave in the basement that includes a fully furnished library, office, gym and theater. You don't have to use Hitler to supplement our income. I don't know what to say about the whole African-American strain of the book. Anyway I love you.

CHAPTER 70

I love you too. There's nothing to say about the African-American strain. It is what it is just as I am what I am and so forth. To be or not to be a Signifyin(g) Monkey—that's what Hamlet really means. That's what everybody means; they just don't know it. In *Hitler: The Terminal Biography*, I am evolving a cult of awareness. My double consciousness, my forked tongue, my synecdochal ears, my penchant for deceit (in the sacred name of truth-telling), and the geometric slope of my pectoral muscles are my simian/signifyin(g) telltales.

CHAPTER 71

I don't know how to respond to that. I will say that there is a dearth of meaningful female characters in your writing, here and elsewhere. But this isn't a real book. The font and the margins are too big and nothing happens.

CHAPTER 72

Things happen in *Hitler: The Terminal Biography*. And you mean something to me. That is, you're a meaningful character. Seriously.

CHAPTER 73

Are you kidding me? You haven't even described me. Physically, emotionally, psychologically, socially. I'm as flat as a character gets.

CHAPTER 74

You're just my type. There. I described you.

CHAPTER 75

Ok. Leave me alone. I'm trying to write a book of my own. A real book. A novel. Do you know how hard that is to do with kids crawling all over you? Your kids, by the way. It would be nice if you could take them to the park once in awhile and give me a little free time. But my expectations are managed. Right now I just want you to quit harassing me. By the way your beans are done.

CHAPTER 76

Thank you. I hope they're not overcooked like last time. They were really mushy and I had to throw them out. Beans are a good pre-workout food. Supplemented with a tablespoon of maple syrup, BCAAs and a protein shake, I have as much energy as a speed fiend at the top of a hill. That reminds me. Could you put the sweet potatoes in the oven when you get a chance? I'd appreciate it. Honey? Did you hear me about the sweet potatoes? Honey? Honey? Don't forget about the sweet potatoes. Honey? Honey? Honey? Honey?

CHAPTER 77

This back-and-forth with my wife has gone all right but obviously I'm forcing things at this point. It has become unsustainable. And Villafuerte is dead. And Hitler is dead. And all of the Jazz Age poets and musicians and flappers and drunks are dead. All that remains is language, which predates humanity in any case. Language is not private. It is public. It is conventional. Everybody owns it. The same might be said for the color of my character. I do not own it. That character belongs to the body of users who perceive and interpret it. Simple mathematics. Hence the terminal crisis of subjectivity and identity with respect to the Dark Hypotenuse, my term for the Lacanian Real, that angry kernel of nothingness around which the world turns. But the Dark Hypotenuse is a topic for another biography. For now, I only ask that you don't get too close to it. Immolation may ensue.

ABOUT THE AUTHOR

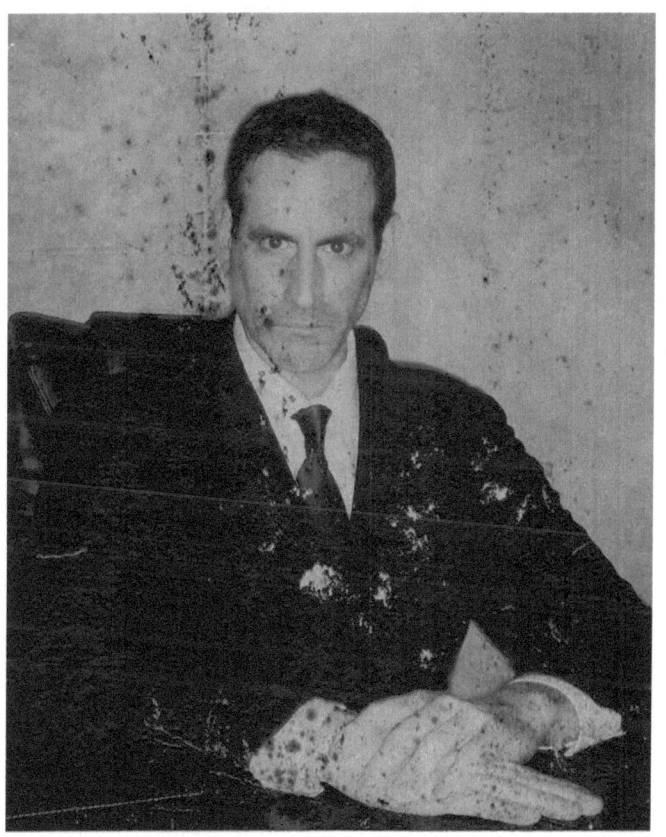

D. HARLAN WILSON is an award-winning, critically acclaimed novelist, short story writer, theorist, editor, historian, publisher and English professor. Visit him online at **DHarlanWilson.com** and **TheKyotoMan.com**.

In this unofficial, unauthorized sequel to Peter Gay's groundbreaking *Freud: A Life of Our Time*, D. Harlan Wilson reveals a side of the man that has proven too disturbing and risqué for past biographers. Based on newly recovered diaries, microfiche, letters, and secret tape recordings, *Freud: The Penultimate Biography* recounts the daring sexual exploits of the father of psychoanalysis. Once considered to be impotent by the age of forty, if only according to the written testimonies of his wife, Freud is now revealed as an uncompromising flâneur, the figurehead of masculine sexuality and phallic prowess that everybody knew he was. It is a dangerous and at times shocking chronicle that puts the very nature of desire on trial.

"Wilson's torrid biography of Sigmund Freud has quickly become my fondest guilty pleasure. And I have many guilty pleasures." **JOHN SAPPINGTON MARMADUKE**, Professor of Psychology and Men's Studies at the University of Fostoria

www.RawDogScreaming.com

Frederick Douglass stands as one of American history's most extraordinary figures, overcoming the evils of slavery and racial construction by force of will and grit. As a fervent abolitionist, gifted orator, and sagacious editor and author, he became one of the most outspoken and influential social reformers of his time. During his life, he published three autobiographies chronicling his struggle from childhood to adulthood, from slave to free man, from ignorance to power-knowledge. And yet the full narrative of the life of Frederick Douglass, contrary to popular belief, has been incomplete . . . until now. Recently recovered on an archeological dig in Ireland, where Douglass lectured extensively in the 1840s, this heretofore "lost" autobiography marks the fourth and final work in the library of his selfhood. Tying together loose ends in the previous three autobiographies while exposing remarkable, often disturbing secrets about his private life, Douglass portrays himself not only as a man of words and character but as a kind of anachronistic hipster and proto-beatnik. There is a reason this volume never saw publication during his lifetime. A reason—and a method.

"Once again, D. Harlan Wilson biographizes with a hammer. Beware." **WILLIAM CLARKE QUANTRILL**, Professor of Religious Studies and Director of the Booker T. Washington Institute for African and African-American Research at the University of Fostoria

www.RawDogScreaming.com